UNI

Uni the UNICORN

and the Butterfly

P9-DCD-289

an Amy Krouse Rosenthal book

pictures based on art by Brigette Barrager

Random House New York

Uni and friends
are playing
on the way to school.

Dear Parents:

Congratulations! Your child is taking the first steps on an exciting journey. The destination? Independent reading!

STEP INTO READING® will help your child get there. The program offers five steps to reading success. Each step includes fun stories and colorful art or photographs. In addition to original fiction and books with favorite characters, there are Step into Reading Non-Fiction Readers, Phonics Readers and Boxed Sets, Sticker Readers, and Comic Readers—a complete literacy program with something to interest every child.

Learning to Read, Step by Step!

Ready to Read   Preschool–Kindergarten
• big type and easy words • rhyme and rhythm • picture clues
For children who know the alphabet and are eager to begin reading.

Reading with Help   Preschool–Grade 1
• basic vocabulary • short sentences • simple stories
For children who recognize familiar words and sound out new words with help.

Reading on Your Own   Grades 1–3
• engaging characters • easy-to-follow plots • popular topics
For children who are ready to read on their own.

Reading Paragraphs   Grades 2–3
• challenging vocabulary • short paragraphs • exciting stories
For newly independent readers who read simple sentences with confidence.

Ready for Chapters   Grades 2–4
• chapters • longer paragraphs • full-color art
For children who want to take the plunge into chapter books but still like colorful pictures.

STEP INTO READING® is designed to give every child a successful reading experience. The grade levels are only guides; children will progress through the steps at their own speed, developing confidence in their reading. The F&P Text Level on the back cover serves as another tool to help you choose the right book for your child.

Remember, a lifetime love of reading starts with a single step!

Text copyright © 2022 by Amy Krouse Rosenthal Revocable Trust
Cover art and interior illustrations copyright © 2022 by Brigette Barrager
Written by Candice Ransom
Illustrations by Lissy Marlin

All rights reserved. Published in the United States by Random House Children's Books, a division of Penguin Random House LLC, New York.

Step into Reading, Random House, and the Random House colophon are registered trademarks of Penguin Random House LLC.

Visit us on the Web!
StepIntoReading.com
rhcbooks.com

Educators and librarians, for a variety of teaching tools, visit us at RHTeachersLibrarians.com

Library of Congress Cataloging-in-Publication Data is available upon request.
ISBN 978-0-593-37775-8 (trade) — ISBN 978-0-593-37776-5 (lib. bdg.) —
ISBN 978-0-593-37777-2 (ebook)

Printed in the United States of America
10 9 8 7 6 5 4 3 2

This book has been officially leveled by using the F&P Text Level Gradient™ Leveling System.

Goldie has his
sparkle ball.

Silky has a
seashell.

Pinkie has a
pink ribbon.

Uni wants something
to play with, too.
Uni looks all around.

Uni sees a
strange object
on a twig.

It looks like a leaf
hanging upside down.

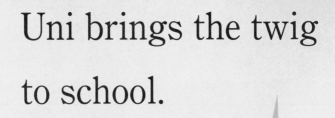

Uni brings the twig
to school.

"That is a chrysalis
on the twig,"
says Mr. Wise.

"A butterfly
will hatch from it."

Uni would love
to have a pet!
Uni decides
to keep the chrysalis.

"Here is a jar
to keep it safe,"
says Uni's mother.

Uni waits and waits.
The chrysalis
slowly changes.

One day,
the chrysalis splits.
The butterfly
pushes its head out.
It is hatching!

Hatching is hard work.

"You can do it!"

Uni cheers.

The butterfly
crawls out
with wet wings.
It does not move.

"My butterfly is not moving," says Uni.

"Its wings need to dry,"
Uni's father says.
"Give it time."

Uni waits while the butterfly's wings dry flat.

Then Uni gives the butterfly
a piece of orange.
The butterfly
likes the juice!

But it does not fly.

Uni takes the jar
to Mr. Wise.
The teacher
is in his garden.

"My pet butterfly
will not fly," says Uni.

"It needs room,"
says Mr. Wise.

"I will get a
bigger jar," Uni says.

"But will your
butterfly be happy?"
Mr. Wise asks.

Uni watches
wild butterflies flutter
around flowers.

Those butterflies
are not in jars.
They are free
and happy.

Uni does not want
an unhappy butterfly.
It should be free, too.

Uni opens the jar.

The butterfly

flies out!

It soars on
strong wings!

The butterfly
seems to wave at Uni.
Uni waves back.

"Goodbye, friend!"

Uni calls.

Uni and the butterfly
both join their friends
to play.